To Frankie Mayhew,
an astro-sir

Astrosaurs ACADEMY

STEVE COLE

VOLCANO INVADERS!

Illustrated by Woody Fox

RED FOX

VOLCANO INVADERS!
A RED FOX BOOK 978 1 862 30887 9

First published in Great Britain by Red Fox,
an imprint of Random House Children's Publishers UK
A Random House Group Company

This edition published 2010

3 5 7 9 10 8 6 4

Copyright © Steve Cole, 2010
Cover illustration and cards by Dynamo Design
© Random House Children's Books, 2010
Map © Charlie Fowkes, 2010
Illustrations copyright © Woody Fox, 2010

Set in 16/20pt Bembo Schoolbook by
Falcon Oast Graphic Art Ltd

Red Fox Books are published by Random House Children's Publishers UK,
61–63 Uxbridge Road, London W5 5SA

www.**randomhousechildrens**.co.uk
www.randomhouse.co.uk

Addresses for companies within The Random House Group Limited can
be found at: www.randomhouse.co.uk/offices.htm

THE RANDOM HOUSE GROUP Limited Reg. No. 954009

A CIP catalogue record for this book is available from
the British Library.

WELCOME TO THE COOLEST SCHOOL IN SPACE . . .

Most people think that dinosaurs are extinct. Most people believe that these weird and wondrous reptiles were wiped out when a massive space rock smashed into the Earth, 65 million years ago.

HA! What do *they* know? The dinosaurs were way cleverer than anyone thought . . .

This is what *really* happened: they saw that big lump of space rock coming, and when it became clear that dino-life could not survive such a terrible crash, they all took off in huge, dung-powered spaceships before it hit.

The dinosaurs set their sights on the stars and left the Earth, never to return . . .

Now, 65 million years later, both plant-eaters and meat-eaters have built massive empires in a part of space called the  Jurassic Quadrant. But the carnivores are never happy unless they're causing trouble. That's why the Dinosaur Space Service needs herbivore heroes to defend the Vegetarian Sector. Such heroes have a special name. They are called ASTROSAURS.

But you can't change from a dinosaur to an astrosaur overnight. It takes years of training on the special planet of Astro

Prime in a *very* special place ... the Astrosaurs Academy! It's a sensational space school where manic missions and incredible adventures are the 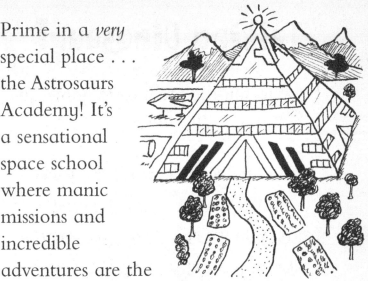 only subjects! The academy's doors are always open, but only to the bravest, boldest dinosaurs ...

And to YOU!

NOTE: One of the most famous astrosaurs of all is Captain Teggs Stegosaur. This staggering stegosaurus is the star of many stories ... But before he became a spaceship captain, he was a cadet at Astrosaurs Academy. These are the adventures of the young Teggs and his friends – adventures that made him the dinosaur he is today!

Talking Dinosaur!

How to say the prehistoric names in this book

DIPLODOCUS – *di-PLOH-de-kus*

PTEROSAUR – *teh-roh-SORE*

STEGOSAURUS – *STEG-oh-SORE-us*

SEISMOSAURUS – *SIZE-moh-SORE-us*

AMMOSAURUS – *AM-oh-SORE-us*

DICERATOPS – *dye-SERRA-tops*

ANKYLOSAUR – *an-KILE-oh-SORE*

DRYOSAURUS – *DRY-oh-SORE-us*

MEGALOSAURUS – *MEG-uh-lo-SORE-us*

The cadets

THE DARING DINOS

Teggs Dutch Blink

DAMONA'S DARLINGS

Damona Netta Splatt

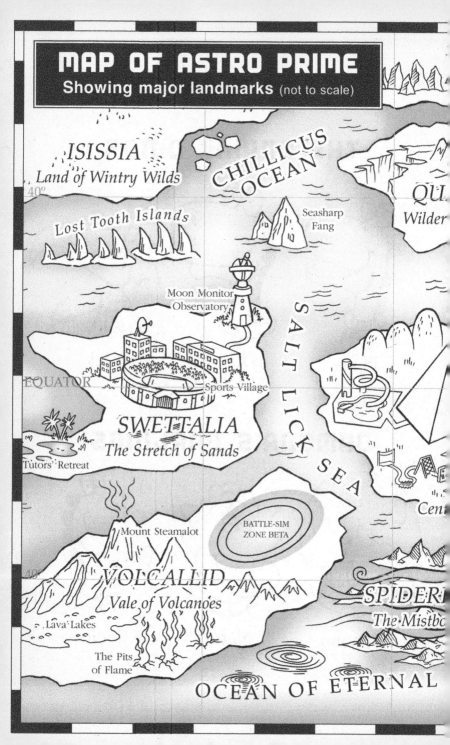

Chapter One

A RECKLESS RACE

"Look out, below!" yelled Teggs Stegosaur, swooping through the sky in a cool new astro-flyer.

Dutch Delaney, a stocky green diplodocus, swerved his speed-car out of the way as Teggs whizzed past. "Don't crash that flyer, dude!" he shouted. "Not before I've had a go in it, anyway!"

Dutch had to swerve again as a yellow pterosaur came bombing past in a low-flying turbo-glider.

"Testing all these different vehicles is brilliant fun!" cried the pterosaur, Blink Fingawing. "I think Pilot Lessons are my favourite thing at Astrosaurs Academy!"

"Mine too," Teggs agreed, performing a perfect loop-the-loop over Blink's glider. "That and the enormous dinners in the canteen."

"And the enormous breakfasts and enormous lunches too," Dutch added, rubbing his tummy. "Not to mention all the other cool lessons . . ."

"And just about everything else!" Teggs said with a grin, as a dozen more young dinosaurs sped past him in other fantastic vehicles.

Teggs was an orange-brown stegosaurus who was determined to be a fully-fledged astrosaur, righting wrongs in outer space. Blink and Dutch were not only his best friends at Astrosaurs Academy, but his team-mates too. They called themselves the Daring Dinos, and had been training hard as astro-cadets for almost two years now.

"Hey, look at that mountain over there," Dutch cried, slowing his speed-car and pointing with his tail. "It's on fire!"

Teggs looked. Right now they were racing round Battle Zone Beta on Volcallid, the hottest, driest continent of Astro Prime.

Further round the coast loomed a vast craggy shape, and Dutch was right – smoke was pouring from the top.

"That's no mountain," brainy Blink informed him, pushing his chunky glasses further up his beak. "That's Mount Steamalot, the biggest volcano in the whole Jurassic Quadrant. I saw a TV show about it. Smoke often comes out of its top, but it hasn't erupted in thousands of years." He frowned. "Mind you, I don't remember it looking quite so smoky before . . ."

"ALL RIGHT, CADETS!" boomed a familiar voice from a rocky plain behind them. It was the Academy's head teacher, Commander Gruff. He was a giant

seismosaurus and he was chomping on a banana as though it were a cigar. "Get back here. *ON THE DOUBLE!*"

"What's he doing here?" Teggs wondered. "Colonel Erick is our flying teacher."

"Let's find out," yelled Dutch, turning his speed-car round. "Last one back's an unhatched egg!"

Laughing and whooping, Teggs and Blink steered their flying machines back towards the rocky plain, where dozens more cadets were already coming in to land.

Colonel Erick, a blue ammosaurus, watched the different dino-landings and made notes. "You're showing excellent control of your crafts," he told them all. "But now we've got a *real* test for you!"

Teggs, Blink and Dutch fell in with the other excited astro-cadets, trailing the commander and Erick as they strode up a nearby hill.

"Commander Gruff is here today to see the brand-new, mark three heli-subs in action," Erick explained.

"They are part helicopter, part submarine—"

"And all brilliant!"

cried a pretty red diceratops, pushing through the line of cadets until she was walking just behind Gruff. "My uncle Hiro is an astrosaur, and he took me to try out a mark *two* heli-sub last Christmas. Of course, he let me drive it and I was fabulous . . ."

Teggs shook his head wearily and chomped on a small, salty plant that was growing at his feet. Damona was his main rival at Astrosaurs Academy. She was smart, brave and strong – but liked to show off about it whenever she got the chance! Her team-mates, Netta and Splatt, stayed close to her, as always.

"I'm so glad we're on your team, Damona," said Netta, a pink ankylosaur with a big tail.

7

"Me too!' Splatt, a speedy green dryosaurus, agreed. "Damona's Darlings are the best!"

"The best at making everyone want to be sick," Dutch said quietly, and Blink and Teggs chuckled.

Erick explained more about the ships as he walked. "The mark three heli-subs have stronger shields than the mark twos, making them our safest short-range ships for combat in the water as well as in the air . . ."

Just then, the ground rumbled and shook. Blink flapped a little way into the air in alarm. "An earthquake!" he declared. The other cadets started to mutter in alarm.

"Stay calm, troops," growled Gruff, holding still until the vibration died away. "There's nothing to worry about. The volcano has been puffing a little more than usual, lately – but our underground scanners predict no earthquakes or volcanic eruptions."

"So, it's perfectly safe," Erick agreed, joining Gruff as he strode off to the top of the hill. "Now then, the heli-subs are parked on the shore here . . ."

The cadets bounded over to see, with Teggs and Damona leading the charge. A whole fleet of giant yellow metal tubes with massive rotor blades was waiting on the beach. "Cool," Teggs breathed.

"They've just been delivered by space-transporter," said Gruff. "And since you've all had a lot of pilot lessons it shouldn't take long for you to master the controls."

Erick nodded. "I'll give you half an hour to practise, then I want you to show the commander what these heli-subs can do – by racing each other through air and sea!"

"*YESSSSSS!*" whooped the cadets, surging onto the shore. As usual, Splatt whizzed ahead of everyone, looking for the shiniest heli-sub. Teggs, Blink and Dutch hopped in the nearest one.

Teggs squeezed into a seat and scanned the controls. "Dutch, you can be the main pilot," he suggested. "I'll be your co-pilot."

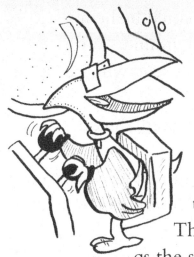

"And I'll control the undersea propellers and the rotors," said Blink happily.

"Works for me, dudes!" Dutch hit the starter button. The engines roared as the smell of burning dung filled the air. "Taking her up!"

But as they rose into the air, another heli-sub went whooshing over their heads. "Hey!" Blink squawked. "Those idiots missed us by a millimetre!"

Teggs saw a familiar red figure at the controls. "Damona's Darlings!"

"Should've known," grumbled Dutch.

Damona's voice crackled through the heli-sub's speakers. "Ready for a race, boys?"

"Erick said we're supposed to practise for half an hour," Blink reminded her.

Netta and Splatt could be heard laughing in the background. "With Damona in the pilot's seat, who needs practice?" said Netta.

"I reckon they're scared," Splatt added.

"Scared?" spluttered Dutch. "Guys, do we dare to take on Damona's Dingbats in a wild heli-sub race?"

Teggs and Blink wasted no time joining in with their traditional battle cry: "WE DARE!"

Dutch pulled on the control stick, Teggs hit the power-boosters and Blink tilted the rotors so they zoomed up into the air, hovering alongside Damona's heli-sub.

"Race you round the coast to Mount Steamalot by air, and back again under the sea," Damona suggested.

"Fine!" Dutch replied.

Teggs looked across at the smouldering Mount Steamalot. Was the top looking a little redder? "I don't know . . . that volcano *does* look smoky."

"Gruff said there was nothing to worry about," said Netta impatiently. "Come on! Get ready, get set – GO!"

"*Waaaaa-hooooooooooo!*" Dutch cried, as he steered the heli-sub away. "These babies can really shift!"

The two rival teams zoomed out over the ocean, leaving the other cadets far behind.

They travelled at top speed, neck-and-neck. Within minutes, the ominous bulk of Mount Steamalot was looming large ahead of them.

"Funny," Teggs murmured. "It seems to be *shaking* . . ."

The next moment, a noise like thunder rumbled through the air. The Daring Dinos gasped as a fresh fountain of thick, stinking black smoke belched out from the top of Mount Steamalot.

"Damona," Teggs snapped into the communicator, "the race is off. Turn back to Zone Beta right now. Gruff was dead wrong – that volcano's about to blow!"

Chapter Two

CAUGHT IN THE FIRE-STORM

"Come off it, Teggs," said Damona over the communicator. "Steamalot's always smoky."

"Besides, we'll be round it and clear again in five minutes," Netta joined in.

Dutch eyed the smoke from the volcano as it turned from black to deep crimson, and gulped. "We may not have five minutes, dudes."

"Not even five seconds!"

yelled Blink as the top of Mount Steamalot suddenly burst apart in a mind-boggling explosion of furious flames! Streams of scalding, white-hot lava burst out of the inferno like deadly missiles.

"Dutch, get us out of here!" Teggs peered through the windows for any sign of Damona, but the sky had become a blazing haze of ash, dust and flying rock. All landmarks, even the sun, had been blotted out. "Quickly!"

"Easier said than done, dude!" Dutch cried as a lump of stone smashed into the Daring Dinos' heli-sub and sent them tumbling. "I'm not even sure which way IS out."

"Damona!" Teggs called anxiously into the communicator. "Netta, Splatt, do you read me?" His only reply was static, and the grating roar of the volcano as it spat more fire and rock into the poisonous air.

"I hope those guys are OK," said Dutch nervously.

"Maybe they're talking to Commander Gruff," Blink suggested.

Teggs nodded. "We should call him too . . ."

But suddenly, a huge spray of boiling lava splashed over the heli-sub and the vehicle's paintwork hissed and bubbled.

"If that lava gets inside the engines, we're finished!" Dutch shouted.

Blink tapped a red cupboard with his beak. "There are emergency jet packs in the back here."

"But we can't jump ship now," said Teggs. "If any of that lava should hit us, it's instant deep-fried dinosaur!"

"Wait a sec," said Dutch. "This thing is a sub as well as a helicopter, right? We can dodge the rocks and lava by diving into the sea."

Even as he spoke, another sizzling dollop of white-hot sludge splashed against the side of the heli-sub. "Do it!" Teggs urged him.

Dutch pulled on the control stick and the speeding craft plunged downwards, spinning as it went. For a few seconds, the smoke cleared. Teggs caught a crazy corkscrew glimpse of coal-black sky, bright white lava and churning orange sea and then – *Ker-SPLASSSH!* – the stricken heli-sub smashed into the foaming waters.

"Switching to propellers," Blink said urgently. "Thank goodness they still work!"

Teggs frowned as he studied the controls. "But the engines are losing power," he said. "Those lava strikes must have damaged them. We don't have enough energy to get back to Gruff and the others!"

Dutch gulped. "Then – what are we going to do?"

POOM! SPLOOM! Huge boulders began to plop into the ocean like ice cubes into a giant drink. "We'll spring a leak for sure if one of those hits us!" Blink squawked.

"Dive down, Dutch!" said Teggs. His mind was racing. How could they possibly survive this disaster? And what had happened to Damona's Darlings?

"Hey, look!" Blink pointed through the dark water. "Something's moving out there . . ."

Teggs angled the headlamps, and saw a large, sleek grey shape heading away from them. "Follow that fish, Dutch!" he cried. "If it lives in these parts, perhaps it knows a place to hide."

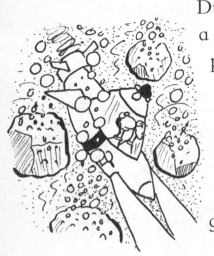

Dutch nodded, hitting a row of switches. "In pursuit!" he announced, steering a path through chunks of sinking stone. "But, um . . . where did it go?"

"There!" Teggs pointed. "There's a kind of undersea cave up ahead."

Blink blinked anxiously as Dutch steered them towards it. "Perhaps we can shelter in there until the eruption stops."

As the heli-sub entered the dark cavern, he saw again the large, grey shape gleaming in the headlights.

"That's no fish, dudes," said Dutch slowly. "It's a vehicle. And I think I recognize it . . ."

Blink gulped. "M-m-m-me too – from space combat lessons."

The strange craft sped away – and as it did so, the headlights uncovered a blood-red sign on its side: a dinosaur skull with rows of jagged teeth.

"That's the mark of meat-eating dinosaurs," said Teggs grimly. "Carnivores have sneaked onto our planet!"

Chapter Three

DANGER ABOVE, MENACE BELOW

High above Teggs and his friends,
Damona, Splatt and Netta were in big
trouble. Damona had tried to steer their
heli-sub into the sea just as Dutch had,
but a massive boulder had smashed into
their rotors and sent them zooming out
of control.

"Hang on,
guys!"
Damona
cried. "This is
going to be
the bumpiest
landing ever –
OOOF!"

Netta and Splatt yelled as the craft scraped and scrunched over the rumbling foothills of Mount Steamalot. The engines cut out. The brakes shrieked in protest.

"Look out!" Splatt yelled as a huge pool of bubbling lava came into sight ahead of them. "If we land in that stuff . . ."

Netta lent her strength to Damona's, pulling hard on the control stick to steer them away. "We can do it," she muttered. "We *must* do it!"

Finally, the battered heli-sub ground to a stop just a few metres from the lava flow. "I hate crash-landings," groaned Damona.

"But now our troubles *really* start," said Netta. The air shimmered with incredible heat, as more rocks came tumbling from the sky, pounding down around them. "We're marooned on an erupting volcano!"

"And no sign of Teggs, Dutch and Blink," said Damona sadly. "Those dino-dimwits drive me crazy, but if anything's happened to them . . ."

"We got lucky. Let's hope they did too." Splatt grabbed the communicator. "Calling Commander Gruff," he said. "Er . . . help?" A distant gravelly voice cut through the static.

"This is Gruff. Are you all OK?"

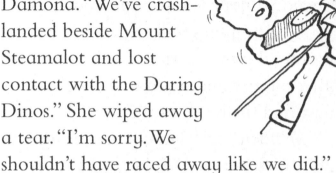

"Not really, sir," said Damona. "We've crash-landed beside Mount Steamalot and lost contact with the Daring Dinos." She wiped away a tear. "I'm sorry. We shouldn't have raced away like we did."

"I shouldn't have told you the volcano was safe," Gruff muttered. "It just doesn't make sense. Volcanoes erupt when red-hot liquid rock bubbles up from the core of the planet – but our scanners have picked up no natural underground activity . . ."

"That's really interesting, sir," squeaked Splatt, as the temperature inside the heli-sub continued to rise. "But can you help us get away from here?"

"I'm working on it," Gruff growled.

"Unfortunately, the volcanic eruption is too fierce for an astro-jet to get through. So Colonel Erick has evacuated your fellow cadets back to the Academy and will return here in an armoured astro-carrier to collect us. No other pilot would stand a chance! You must find shelter until then."

"We'll try," said Damona, peering out into the fire-storm. "Splatt, get the jet packs. Perhaps we will spot Teggs and his team from the air."

"I hope so, troops," the commander told them. "Hang in there. Gruff out."

The communicator went silent. But then, as Splatt yanked opened the heli-sub's supply cupboard, it crackled back into life. "Hello? Any dudes out there listening?"

Netta beamed. "It's Dutch!"

Damona leaned up close to the communicator. "Dutch, where are you? Are the others all right?"

"Damona!" the diplodocus cried. "Never thought I'd say it, but good to hear your voice!"

"We're in an underwater cave beneath the volcano," chirped Blink.

"Are *you* guys all OK?" Teggs added.

A gigantic boulder smashed down just beside Damona's Darlings' wrecked ship. "We won't be for long if we stick around here!" Damona said as she, Splatt and Netta struggled into their jet packs. "Gruff is sending help, and we're

going to search for shelter on the
surface. Can you hold out down there?"

"I hope so," said Teggs. "We think
we've spotted a carnivore Fly-Diver
scout ship!"

Damona frowned. "You've spotted a
what?"

Splatt kicked open the buckled doors
and bundled Netta outside. "Come on,
Damona!"

"Wait," Damona
said urgently. "You
really think there are
carnivores about,
Teggs?"

"It might be just an
old wreck left over
from one of the
Raptor Wars," Teggs
admitted. "We're going
to see. But just in case anything happens
. . . I hope you know we were beating
you in that race!"

"You wish!" Damona smiled, despite the situation. "Bye, Teggs. And if you do find any meat-eaters, save some for us to fight!"

Then she ran outside into the fiery heat, switched on her jet pack and soared away with her friends into the stinking, smoke-filled sky, looking for 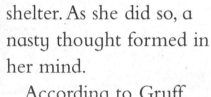 shelter. As she did so, a nasty thought formed in her mind.

According to Gruff, the planet's scanners had picked up no natural underground activity that could have caused Mount Steamalot to erupt. And now Teggs, Dutch and Blink had spotted a carnivore ship underneath the volcano . . .

Could the two events be connected?

Deep down beneath the sea, Teggs,
Dutch and Blink were searching for the
mysterious ship. The rocky caverns
seemed to stretch on for ever. There were
no fish or weeds or any
sign of life at all. Only
darkness.

Teggs shivered, glad of the company
of his friends. It was a frightening
feeling to be cut off from the world
above, drifting through the unknown.

"Hey, what's that?" Blink pointed his
wing at two faint red lights shining
above them through the bubbling murk.

"Checking it out," Dutch murmured,
steering upwards.

To Teggs's surprise, the heli-sub suddenly burst out of the water into thick, smoky darkness. "Whoa!" Dutch cried, switching off the engine. They stayed floating like a rubber duck in a giant bath – and the headlights picked out a stretch of dark, volcanic ground ahead of them, with rough walls of stone beyond.

"Well, we've *sort of* reached the surface," said Blink nervously. "Or ground level at any rate. This must be a secret cave leading inside the volcano."

"And those are the lights we saw . . ." Through a side-window, Teggs pointed to the glowing red dots that had led them here, now just a stone's throw away.

"Rear parking lamps," Blink observed. "So that Fly-Diver *isn't* a wreck. It was steered here on purpose."

Dutch scowled. "A big volcano erupts without warning and we find some crummy carnivores on the scene. I'm no genius, but I'm guessing there's a link."

"Why else would they be here if not to cause trouble," agreed Blink. "Meat-eaters are always trying to invade the Vegetarian Sector."

"And astrosaurs always stop them," said Teggs. "Let's put on the jet packs and take a closer look." As he wriggled into his harness and Dutch did the same, Blink flicked a switch and the roof flipped open. They flew out through the smoky darkness to where the

Fly-Diver stood parked on the rocky, underground shore, and grabbed torches from their belts.

"Hey, the ground's covered in ash," Blink noted as he flapped down beside Teggs. "And there are tracks."

Teggs studied the enormous footprints in the ash. "From the size of these claws, we're dealing with one of the larger carnivore breeds . . ."

Blink gulped. "Oh, good!"

"However big they are," Dutch whispered, "we have to follow them." He held out his hand. "Do we dare?"

Blink and Teggs put their hands on his. "We dare!" they hissed.

Then Teggs led his friends into the hot, stifling darkness . . .

Chapter Four

THE CARNIVORES

The Daring Dinos followed the trail of footprints through a big, winding tunnel. It grew hotter and hotter. High above them, the rocky roof glowed red with the amazing heat. "I think we're heading towards the heart of the volcano," Blink whispered.

As they rounded a corner, the tunnel opened up into a giant

cave. There were hundreds of holes in every wall, like a kind of volcanic honeycomb. But then Teggs suddenly stopped dead. Dutch and Blink peered past him – and soon saw the reason why.

Two enormous dark-red dinosaurs in blue overalls, with huge teeth, powerful arms and vicious claws, stood in the middle of the cave. Luckily, they had their backs to Teggs and his friends. In the pale light of a large electric lantern they were studying a collection of weird-looking metal gadgets laid out on the ground.

Teggs led Dutch and Blink over to hide behind a nearby boulder. Dutch shuddered. "Those suckers are even bigger than T. rexes!"

"They look like a pair of megalosaurus to me," Blink whispered. "From the planet Megalos."

The megalosaurus monsters started fitting the gadgets together to make a larger machine.

"What's that they're building?" Teggs wondered. "It looks like a weapon."

"What if it's some kind of volcano-bomb?" Dutch gasped. "Maybe that's why Mount Steamalot started erupting, even though Gruff said it couldn't!"

"And this volcano is big enough to

affect the whole planet." Blink's eyelids fluttered wildly. "Everyone on Astro Prime is in danger!"

"We've got to stop those monsters before they can do any more damage," Teggs muttered, holding out his hand. "I know we've asked this a lot today, but . . . do we dare?"

With brave smiles, Dutch and Blink braced themselves for battle and placed their hands on his. "*WE DAAAAAAAARRRRRRRE!*" The three cadets' war cry rang out through the cavern as they charged at the carnivores.

The two megalosaurus turned in surprise. "Plant-eaters!" gasped the biggest.

"That's us!" Whirling his tail high above his head, Teggs whacked the biggest carnivore in the chops with its bony tip. "And it looks like you're *tail*-eaters!"

"Not to mention *foot-eaters*," Dutch added. He did a handstand, kicked the second megalosaurus with his back legs and knocked him flying. But the first had already recovered from

Teggs's blow and opened its jaws wide in warning. Blink cheekily flapped up and pecked its tongue with his beak. The carnivore howled with pain.

The smaller megalosaurus lunged for Blink. But the plucky dino-bird gave it a double wing-slap, and Teggs and Dutch followed up with a pair of punches that knocked the monster to its knees.

"Wait!" cried the biggest carnivore in a booming voice. It held up both hands and stuck out its sore tongue. "We have no quarrel with you."

"Oh, really?" Teggs glared at it. "Well, maybe *we* have a quarrel with carnivores causing our biggest volcano to erupt!"

"You think *we* are to blame?" The other megalosaurus snorted. "You plant-eaters must be even bigger twerps than we thought!"

"Oh, sure," Blink jeered. "You're totally innocent."

Dutch folded his arms. "I suppose you just wandered into a live volcano in the Vegetarian Sector looking for a guided tour, huh?"

"I am Tarq," said the smaller megalosaurus, turning to his friend. "And this is Korlius. We wear the blue overalls of scientists, not the crimson armour of warriors."

"How did you get past our defences?" Teggs demanded.

"We sneaked our ship on board a

space transporter delivering mark three heli-subs," Tarq admitted. "Then we switched on the heli-subs' super-strong shields so our own Fly-Diver beside them was not detected."

"Clever," Blink admitted. "And very sneaky."

"But we are not here to invade," Korlius insisted. "We have come in the hope of saving millions of dinosaurs – both our kind and yours – from a terrible enemy."

Teggs frowned. "What are you on about?"

Korlius took up the story. "Two weeks ago our armies tested their latest big weapons on Malga, the moon of Megalos. Soon after, a large volcano there erupted. We thought perhaps the weapon had set it off . . . until that same volcano *took off* from Malga and attacked our planet without warning!"

Teggs, Dutch and Blink spoke together: "*What?*"

"The volcano fired lava-lasers at our biggest cities," Tarq went on. "It was actually a *spaceship* in disguise – a spaceship controlled by volcano-men made of living, fiery rock."

"We're too old for fairy stories, dude," Dutch retorted.

"The volcano-men are no fairy story," Korlius assured him. "They are a legend from the distant past, now returned to brutal, rocky life."

"And Mount Steamalot is another of their secret spaceships!" Tarq looked around nervously as more shockwaves rumbled through the cavern. "What's happening here is no ordinary volcanic eruption. It is the volcano-men starting up their engines and clearing out the lava from their control rooms!"

"A volcano spaceship?" Teggs felt a shiver run down his spiky backbone, despite the heat. "You mean this whole place could soon be lifting off?"

Dutch gulped. "With us on board!"

"It's too astonishing for words!" squawked Blink. "Although thinking about it, all that smoke coming out of Mount Steamalot over the centuries *could* be due to a dodgy exhaust pipe! And those holes in the walls over there look like they were drilled – perhaps for running power cables right through a rocky space-base."

"Precisely," said Tarq gravely.

"But how can they have been hidden here for so long?" Teggs argued. "They'd have to be hundreds of years old."

"*Thousands*," Korlius corrected him. "Maybe even millions. Rock lasts for ever!"

"I remember hearing stories of the volcano-men when I was just a  hatchling." Blink perched on the carnivores' half-built machine. "The legends say they lived in the Jurassic Quadrant long before the dinosaurs came here – but they were all destroyed in a big space war with a race of water-warriors."

"*Almost* all of them," said Tarq. "We scientists have been looking into it. We think the volcano-men knew that they were losing that war. So their king and his remaining soldiers decided to hibernate inside their secret volcano ships, right across the Quadrant. They hid themselves in lava, planning to rise and launch surprise attacks on their watery foes when reinforcements arrived."

Korlius nodded. "Those reinforcements were supposed to send a wake-up signal . . . But they were wiped out by the water-warriors before they could."

"The king and his hidden armies went on sleeping for thousands and thousands of years," Tarq explained. "In the meantime, the water-warriors moved to another galaxy to fight other wars . . . and we dinosaurs came to the Jurassic Quadrant."

Teggs looked around nervously.

47

"Never guessing what was lurking out of sight . . ."

Suddenly, an even larger tremor shook the cavern. Korlius grabbed hold of Tarq's claw. "Enough talk. We must hurry. The volcano-men could wake up at any moment."

"Um, I've got news for you, dude." Dutch gulped and pointed across the cave. "They already have!"

Teggs and Blink whirled round to find a sinister figure watching them from the other side of the cave. It seemed to be made of stone. Its body was a large, round boulder, and its head was cone-shaped, like a mini volcano. Its arms and legs were like big rocky beads, threaded on an invisible rope. Its slit-like eyes glowed red-hot. Smoke hissed from its mouth.

"Intruders!" screamed the creature. It opened its mouth to reveal teeth like stone axe-heads and clenched its glowing fists. "Attack!"

Chapter Five

THE HEAT OF BATTLE

"Incoming!" Dutch cried as the creature lurched towards them.

Korlius charged at the volcano-man – but with a sharp nod of its head, the monster spat a blazing ball of lava at his chest that knocked him to the ground.

Teggs ran forward, tail raised, and landed a heavy blow on the volcano-man's head. But it only roared and punched him with a scorching hot fist.

Teggs gasped and staggered backwards.

Blink, meanwhile, had taken to the air. "There's a crack in the ground beneath that thing!" he cried. "Dutch, Tarq, if you smack down your tails really hard . . ."

"On the case, dude," Dutch yelled. "Come on, meat-breath – one, two, *THREE!*"

The volcano-man pounded towards them but Dutch and Tarq's double tail-strike was already hammering down with incredible force. The ground shook and split open beneath the volcano-man, who disappeared into darkness. A noisy *splash* soon followed as he hit the waters below.

"Good work, guys," said Teggs shakily.

"Now we must hurry," grunted Korlius, limping back to the machine. "We have little time. That was only the first of thousands – one of the servants who will prepare the ship for take-off before his masters wake."

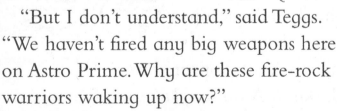

"But I don't understand," said Teggs. "We haven't fired any big weapons here on Astro Prime. Why are these fire-rock warriors waking up now?"

"The volcano-men of Malga wiped

out a quarter of our entire population before we stopped them at our north pole," Tarq hissed. "They couldn't stand the cold. But before they froze, they sent a wake-up call to their king and his army, urging him to rouse his forces and destroy all dinosaurs!"

"We traced the signal through space," explained Korlius. "It went right here to this volcano – and now the king has awoken."

Teggs gasped. "The king of the volcano-men is here on Astro Prime?"

Tarq nodded. "When their hidden spaceship is fully charged and ready to fly, they will destroy this planet and move on to others . . . conquering plant-eaters and meat-eaters alike."

"Why didn't you warn us?" cried Blink.

"Would your leaders have believed such a fantastic story?" Tarq sneered. "I doubt it. Besides, warning puny leaf-munchers of danger would ruin our reputation as evil baddies!"

"And in any case," said Korlius, "we can vanquish the king and his rock-warriors simply and peacefully if we can stop them before they wake."

"And I know how!" Blink turned knowingly to the carnivores. "This gadget you're building . . . is it by any chance a sub-zero mega ice-maker?"

Tarq looked surprised. "Exactly right. It turns any liquid into an icy sludge."

"It should put out the fires of Mount Steamalot for ever," Korlius added. "We have already frozen two other volcano ships in this way."

"Then let's call a truce and work together to get this mega ice-maker on the go," Teggs declared, as the strongest tremor yet rocked the volcano. "We can't afford to waste any more time."

"I'm quite good with machines," said Blink, already sorting through the metal parts on the ground. "I just hope the volcano-men don't start attacking before we've finished!"

"We must hurry," agreed Tarq. "Korlius, show the big, juicy leaf-munchers how to build the deep-freeze element. The crunchy yellow flying thing can help me build the core of the ice-maker . . ."

Teggs, Blink and Dutch did as the megalosaurus told them, putting

together electronic bits and pieces they
barely understood. Sweat poured down
their faces, and their hearts thumped
louder with every shudder and rumble
from the volcano around them. Teggs
kept glancing up to check no other
volcano-men were creeping up on them.
Surely the one who'd fallen through the
crack would soon be missed . . . ?

"Shame these ice-makers don't come
ready-made," Dutch said.

"The core of the machine is too
cold," Tarq explained. "It would freeze
the machine before we could use it!"

Korlius nodded. "But now it is
complete, we will launch it up into the
heart of the volcano so it can do its
work . . ."

"I don't think so!" came a booming cry from above.

Teggs gasped as three figures zoomed out of the shadows . . .

It was Damona – with Netta and Splatt!

Propelled by her jet pack, the red diceratops swooped down at Tarq and Korlius. "We'll teach you meat-loving maniacs to force our friends into helping you!" *WHAM!* She stomped on Tarq with all four of her feet.

"No, Damona!" Teggs yelled. "You don't understand . . ." But he was drowned out by Splatt and Netta yelling as they dropped down to attack Korlius. The carnivore swiped at them with his vicious claws and knocked

Splatt flying before Netta conked him on the head with her club-like tail.

Dutch reared up into the air and grabbed her. "What are you doing, you dippy diplodocus?" she cried.

"Leave the meatheads alone," Dutch shouted, as Teggs and Blink grabbed hold of Splatt.

Netta struggled to get free. "Damona, help! Those monsters must have turned the Daring Dinos bad!"

"It's not that," Teggs protested, as Tarq lunged at Damona, jaws snapping.

She dodged clear and grabbed the mega ice-maker. "I don't know what this thing is meant to do, but it doesn't look friendly!"

"Please, Damona." Blink flapped frantically over. "Put it down!"

"That's just what I plan to do," the diceratops declared – and with all her strength, she smashed the device against the wall!

"*Noooooooooooooooooooooo!*" yelled Teggs, Blink and Dutch. Tarq and Korlius howled in dismay as sparks flew from the mega ice-maker and parts pinged everywhere. But Damona wasn't finished. She hurled the remains into the jagged hole in the ground the volcano-man had fallen through, and – *SPLOOSH!* The machine was lost beneath the bubbling subterranean sea.

"Our only way of stopping the volcano-men," Tarq sobbed. "Gone!"

Chapter Six

THE COMING OF THE VOLCANO-MEN

As the two megalosaurus stared helplessly at the hole in the ground, Splatt and Netta dragged Teggs, Blink and Dutch over to Damona.

"Are you three OK now?" Damona asked as she landed lightly.

Teggs groaned. "Oh, Damona . . . thanks to you, no one on the planet is OK!"

"You're not making any sense," said Damona crossly. "Come on, we'll talk later."

"How did you even find us?" Dutch wondered.

"We found a crack in the volcano and tried to shelter inside," said Splatt.

"Then we found it led to a tunnel!" said Netta. "We thought we could hear your voices echoing from the other end . . ."

Damona nodded. "And since you'd said there might be carnivores about, we wanted to help you squish them!"

Teggs shook his head sadly. "The megalosaurus aren't the bad guys here . . ."

"But THEY are!"

Blink pointed to the other side of the cavern as two enormous rock-monsters with glowing orange eyes came stamping into sight. Lava drooled from their red-hot mouths at the sight of the dinosaurs. Two more of the volcano-men lumbered after them. And then two more . . .

Damona turned pale in terror. "What are those things?"

"Angry volcano-men, the first of thousands," wailed Korlius. "And you have just destroyed the only thing that could have stopped them!"

"Intruders!" roared the volcano-men at the front of the line, pointing at the dinosaurs. "Attack! Attack!"

Netta gulped as the creatures clomped towards them. "Not very friendly, are they?"

"They're deadly," Teggs told her. "And this whole volcano is their spaceship!"

"Their *what*?" Damona smacked a

hand against her
forehead. "Oh, no.
What have I done?"

Splatt groaned.
"Why did I even
get out of bed
today?"

"Jet packs,
everybody,"
Damona cried as the volcano-men drew
closer. "Quickly!"

Netta and Splatt followed her lead
and rose into the air. Blink flapped up
to join them, but Teggs pointed to Tarq
and Korlius. "They don't *have* any jet
packs!"

"They're carnivores!" Netta retorted.
"Let them take care of themselves."

"They were trying to take care of
those monsters!" Teggs shouted. "We
can't just leave them!" He grabbed Tarq
while Dutch took hold of Korlius – and
then both plant-eaters used their jet

64

packs to rise into the air. Korlius was heavier, so Blink helped Dutch carry him.

"Catch the intruders!" hissed the volcano-men. More and more thumped into sight. "Attack! Attack! Send them to Inferniak!"

Blink gulped. "I don't like the sound of that!"

"We'd better get out of here." Damona zoomed towards one of the holes in the high roof of the cavern.

But then a volcano-man pushed its head out from inside! "Catch! Attack!"

65

Damona gasped and twisted aside in mid air as the monster spat a ball of lava straight at her. "Whoa!"

"Hey, dude!" Dutch broke off a stalactite from the cave roof and shoved it into the volcano-man's mouth. "Don't you know it's rude to spit?"

The rock-monster made no answer, clutching its throat as it fell and crashed to the ground below. But its friends soon helped it up. "Inferniak must have them!" the creatures chanted. "Send them to him!"

Splatt vanished up another hole in the ceiling. "This way looks clear!" he shouted. "Come on!"

Teggs, still carrying Tarq, followed Splatt into the narrow stone tunnel. The others were close behind. Thick power cables stretched along the walls of black rock, giving off a dull light and proving to Teggs that the whole volcano had been turned into some fantastic alien vessel thousands of years ago.

"I'm sorry I broke that device," Damona whispered, her voice echoing back at her. "I thought I was saving the planet."

"Instead you have doomed it," Tarq snapped.

"No one's doomed yet," said Teggs. "I wonder where this tunnel leads?"

"To the outside, I hope," Splatt called.

"It's getting hotter," Blink panted, trying to fan himself with his wings as he flew.

Korlius nodded, still holding onto Dutch's legs. "We must be going deeper *into* the volcano."

"Splatt," Teggs called, "if you see another tunnel leading to the right, let's take it."

"There's one up ahead," Splatt reported back. "*Aaargh!*" He swerved aside and everyone gasped as another volcano-man stuck out its big, cone-shaped head to block the way. Netta jetted through the air and clobbered the monster with her hefty tail. Bone struck stone with a grating screech – and the volcano-man fell backwards into the darkness of the tunnel.

"Thanks, Netta," Splatt muttered as the tunnel widened around them and it got hotter still. "This place is a nightmare."

"You think so?" boomed a deep and terrible voice from somewhere up above them. "*I'll* give you a nightmare!"

Suddenly, a fantastic, burning-hot, super-sized fist closed about the group of dinosaurs. Terrified, Teggs fought to stop the grip from tightening – but it wasn't easy while carrying Tarq, and with horror Teggs felt his jet pack crumple against the searing hot stone.

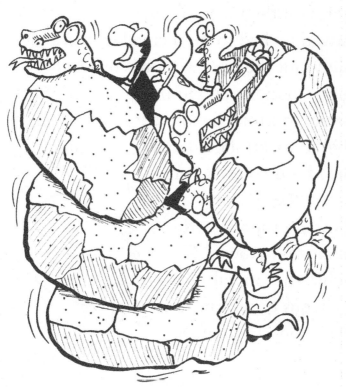

Tarq and Netta squirmed helplessly beside him in the giant fist as it carried them out of the tunnel and into a smoky, wide-open space. Damona, Korlius, Blink and Dutch strained with all their strength to force the fingers apart, but it was no good. All eight dinosaurs were helpless prisoners in a cage of stone.

And as the fist carried them up through the thick air, they realized it was attached to an incredible arm . . . and that the arm was attached to a mind-bogglingly big body . . . and that sitting on top of those extraordinarily broad rocky shoulders was a gigantic head – a colossal cone of stone the size of a house – topped with a blazing crown of white-hot metal.

Teggs gasped in fear and amazement.

The giant monster's eyes were like gaping pits of orange fire. Smoke curled from its huge split of a mouth as it sneered down at its helpless prisoners.

"I am Inferniak," the giant monster boomed. "King of the volcano-men!"

Chapter Seven

CRUSHED BY THE KING!

"Pleased to meet you, your majesty," gasped Teggs, struggling for breath. Looking past Inferniak's enormous head, he could see rows and rows of volcano-men in the open space, standing on wide ledges built into the rough rock walls.

They were working strange controls that dripped with lava, seemingly carved out of the glowing stone. And high above, through thick smoke and ash, he thought he caught a glimpse of daylight. "Nice control room you have here."

Blink nodded, gazing around with keen interest. "It must have been buried beneath molten lava," he said. "Those eruptions we flew through were simply the volcano-men clearing that lava out of the way so Inferniak could move again and get his instruments working."

"Told you so," Tarq muttered.

"No wonder this place has stayed hidden for thousands of years," said Teggs. "Only volcano-creatures could possibly get to the controls."

"Silence, dinosaur," rumbled Inferniak.

Damona stared up at the rocky ruler. "You know about dinosaurs?"

"How else would I be able to speak your language?"

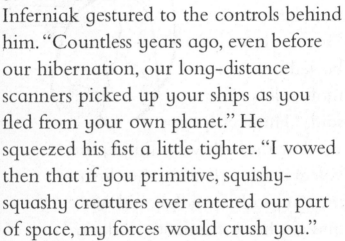

Inferniak gestured to the controls behind him. "Countless years ago, even before our hibernation, our long-distance scanners picked up your ships as you fled from your own planet." He squeezed his fist a little tighter. "I vowed then that if you primitive, squishy-squishy creatures ever entered our part of space, my forces would crush you."

"But . . . this isn't your part of space any more, king dude," Dutch argued. "You fell asleep or whatever. The place was empty, so dinosaurs took over."

"Finders keepers," Tarq agreed.

"What's this?" Inferniak brought his frightening fist closer to his face. "Plant-eating dinosaurs and flesh-eating dinosaurs – together?"

Blink nodded quickly. "Along with bug-crunching winged types like me!"

"Our races will all join forces to defeat you," Teggs warned him.

"I am sure they will try," Inferniak scoffed, squeezing harder.

The helpless dinosaurs gasped in his burning grip. Dutch and Damona's jet packs sparked as they crumpled and broke. Splatt and Netta's packs soon buckled too.

"Go ahead – squish us and roast us," Tarq cried. "We don't care!"

Splatt squeaked. "Speak for yourself!"

"YOU will speak to ME." Inferniak licked his lips with a huge, sandpapery tongue and breathed thick, choking smoke over his captives. "I wish to know the secrets of your dinosaur race. How strong are your armies?"

"Not as strong as our handies," Teggs joked bravely.

Inferniak scowled. "What weapons do you have?"

"I've got a pea-shooter," said Dutch.

The great king's eyes narrowed to fiery slits. "How great are your numbers?"

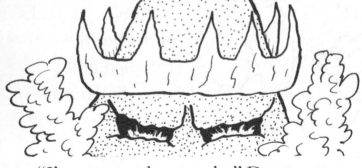

"I'm no good at maths," Damona joined in. "I can tell you about our letters, though."

"You are trying my patience, fools!" the craggy king bellowed. "Answer my questions. What are your weaknesses?"

"I'll tell you . . ." Netta took a deep breath. "I can't resist grass-flavoured chocolates."

"That does it." Smoke came pouring from the top of Inferniak's head. "If you will not give me information, you are of no use to me. I shall crush all your armies in any case!" He sniggered, a sound like a landslide. "We shall rise up in our ship and roam this world, destroying all in our path with our lava-lasers. We shall travel through space and wake my other stone subjects from their long sleep. Then we shall take back every planet we have lost, and hundreds more besides!"

Teggs glared defiantly up at the king. "You won't win. We'll find a way to stop you."

"I think not." Inferniak drew back his fist like an archer making ready to let loose an arrow. "Farewell, puny ones. *BE GONE!*"

And with that, he hurled the dinosaurs away through the clouds of thick smoke, out through the very top of the volcano!

"*Whoaaaa!*" Dutch yelled, somersaulting through the air far above the ocean.

Blink
spread his
wings, trying to get
his crazy flight under
control. "Well, we did want to get
out of Mount Steamalot . . ."

"Oh, yes," groaned Damona dizzily.
"It's a real wish come true."

"Everyone link tails," Teggs
commanded, taking hold of Damona's
before she hurtled out of reach. "It will
stop us falling too far away from each
other."

"What's the use?" Splatt stared through the smoke at the ocean far below as it began to get closer. "Beak-brain's OK, he can fly – but with our jet packs broken, the rest of us don't stand a chance."

"DO IT!" Teggs insisted. Damona grabbed Dutch. Dutch put his arms around Netta, who clutched Splatt to her like a big teddy bear.

Tarq and Korlius clung together as they fell like formation skydivers. Teggs reached out and grabbed Korlius by the tail. "We're still in this together," he shouted. "Blink, is there any way you can keep us in the air?"

Blink took hold of Tarq's tail and strained upwards with all his power. "No . . . good . . ." he grunted. "Together . . . you're too heavy . . ."

Tarq shook his head as the air whistled around them. "You are brave, plant-eaters," he admitted. "But bravery cannot save us now."

"Maybe not!" Netta gasped, suddenly lurching unsteadily upwards. "But perhaps one battered jet pack can!"

"Yes!" cried Teggs. "We still have a chance! If you and Blink can only slow down our fall . . ."

Korlius shook his head. "Even if they can, we are too far from land to swim for safety."

"Oh, stop your moaning!" said Damona, clinging onto Dutch as they continued to plummet. "We've been in worse scrapes than this."

"Right," Dutch agreed. "I just can't remember any!"

Splatt covered his eyes. "We're going to hit! We're going to hit any second!"

"Come on, Blink," Netta screamed, setting her jet-pack controls to maximum. "Give it all you've got!"

"I am!" Blink flapped his wings so fast they were a leathery blur. "I *am!*"

Teggs gritted his teeth and tightened his grip on Damona and Korlius as they plunged the final distance and the sea came rushing up to meet them . . .

Chapter Eight

LANDING FOR TAKE-OFF!

Closing his eyes, still dropping from the sky at alarming speed, Teggs braced himself for the mother of all splashes . . .

But instead – *SLUSSSHHH!*

The landing was cold but surprisingly soft. Teggs had expected to fall down, down through the ocean waters, but instead had only sunk a few metres.

Because the sea wasn't simply water any more. It was slushy and half frozen, like a vast field of orange ice cream, stretching over to the ominous coast of Volcallid and the smoking cone of Mount Steamalot.

"What the . . . ?" Teggs helped a dazed Damona climb out of the pit she had smashed into the half-frozen sea. With a surge of relief he saw Dutch, Blink and the carnivores climbing to their feet too. Netta rose up out of another hole in the icy slush, holding onto Splatt.

Then, with a splutter and a pop, her jet pack finally died and they dropped down beside Tarq and Korlius.

"What's happened to the ocean?" asked Splatt in wonder.

Blink's eyes were gleaming. "It can only be the carnivores' sub-zero mega ice-maker."

Damona stared at him. "That machine in the cave, you mean? I thought I'd smashed it!"

"You did – but you must have accidentally activated its ice-core before you threw it into the sea," Tarq realized. "It was meant to freeze the heart of the volcano to seal the volcano-men inside. Now, instead, it is trying to freeze this entire ocean!"

"Awesome!" Dutch beamed. "We can skate home and raise the alarm!"

"I fear that will not be possible," said Korlius. "The ice-maker was not designed to freeze something as vast as the sea. Soon it will overload and blow itself to bits!"

"And the frozen ocean will explode too!" Blink groaned. "Think of those icy tidal waves . . ."

Damona nodded. "But King Inferniak will just take off in his volcano ship and rise up above it all."

"Blink," said Teggs urgently, "you must fly to Commander Gruff and tell him what's happening."

Blink stared. "But I can't leave you all here to be blown up!"

"You must, dude," Dutch urged him.

"Otherwise the whole Jurassic Quadrant will fry for sure!"

Blink opened his beak to reply – but then the solid water around them began to rumble and shake.

"What's that?"

Teggs looked at Tarq in alarm. "Is it the ice-core, getting ready to overload?"

"No!" Netta pointed to Mount Steamalot. "It's *that*!"

The cadets and their sharp-toothed visitors stared in awe and alarm as a thick, horizontal split opened up around the base of the giant volcano. Solid rock tore apart with a deafening rumble that made the loudest thunderclap sound like a baby's whisper. Lava, smoke and ash exploded from the split as – incredibly, impossibly – the volcano began to rise slowly into the air.

"This is *so* not good!" Damona hung her head. "Inferniak's leaving, and any minute now we'll be blown sky-high!"

Tarq and Korlius burst into tears. "The Jurassic Quadrant is doomed!"

"Not just yet, it's not," Teggs shouted as a huge shadow fell over them. "Look!"

The astounding racket of the lifting volcano had drowned out the approach of an enormous Academy astro-carrier! As the giant vessel hovered in the smoky air above them, two familiar faces appeared at the window.

"Commander Gruff! Colonel Erick!" Blink did a fluttery somersault. "Thank goodness!"

Damona grinned. "Gruff *said* he'd get us out of here!"

Gruff stretched his neck out of the window, looking baffled and alarmed.

"We came to rescue you – but just what in the world is happening? The sea's freezing to slush, Mount Steamalot is taking off . . ."

Erick's eyes widened at the sight of Tarq and Korlius. "And there are carnivore invaders on Astro Prime!"

"It's the *volcano* invaders we have to worry about, sir!" Dutch called.

"That and the whole sea exploding," Splatt added, jumping up and down as if trying to reach the astro-carrier. "Please, Commander, get us out of here!"

"I'll let down the astro-lift," shouted Erick, and a metal platform appeared, lowered on metal chains from a hatchway in the belly of the ship.

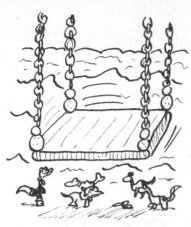

Gruff's eyes were on stalks as the volcano turned slowly onto its side in mid air, white-hot jets firing from its base. "I think you'd better tell us everything."

"No time, sir," said Teggs breathlessly. "I've got a plan. Do you have long-range weapons on board?"

"No," said Gruff. "I wasn't expecting a fight."

"We can't risk getting too close to Inferniak . . ." Teggs frowned. "Hey. Where are all the other heli-subs?"

"In the cargo bay at the back of this ship," called Erick.

"Fabulous!" Teggs punched the air.

"Our only chance to stop the biggest mega disaster in dinosaur history is to steer all the heli-subs on autopilot straight into the sides of Mount Steamalot."

"What?" Erick looked shocked. "Turn all those lovely, brand-new vessels into scrap?"

"We can't attack a giant, flying volcano with a handful of heli-subs, cadet," Gruff protested. "That's like attacking a raptor Death Ship with a drawing pin!"

"Teggs has flipped," Splatt declared, scrambling onto the carrier's astro-lift as the sea itself started to tremble. "Come on, this slushy sea will explode at any moment."

"Which is precisely why we have to lure Inferniak over here," Teggs cried. "Huge amounts of ice are the one thing that might stop him before he starts destroying the planet."

"Of course!" Damona nodded. "He's right, Commander. Sending little ships crashing into his *big* ship might get his attention and bring him over here to investigate."

Netta gulped. "So either he will destroy us, or the exploding ocean will!"

Blink was thinking hard, his eyelids blinking away. "The volcano ship is huge and heavy – it won't be able to dodge the blast. But the astro-carrier is smaller and lighter . . ."

Erick sighed and nodded. "I guess it might just out-race the shockwave."

Teggs nodded eagerly. "It will with you flying it, sir!"

"Ultra-risky, but worth a try," Dutch agreed, holding out his hand. "Do we dare?"

The Daring Dinos put their hands together. Damona and Netta put their hands on top, and even Tarq and Korlius hurried to join in. With a sigh, Splatt stretched down his tail to complete the vow: "WE DARE!"

"I have no idea what's going on, cadets," Gruff admitted. "But this is clearly an emergency, and you're the Academy's finest. Go to it, troops."

"To the heli-subs!" Teggs cried, leaping onto the platform.

The volcano was slowly turning in a circle, as though Inferniak was looking all around and deciding which part of the planet to devastate first . . .

"We must send those heli-subs crashing into the volcano ship," Teggs went on. "There's not a single second to lose!"

Chapter Nine

MELTDOWN!

On board the volcano ship, Inferniak was studying his instruments and listening to his smaller chief give a report on the planet.

"Life-scanners show only a few thousand dinosaur creatures living here," hissed the chief. "Most of them have gathered at the centre of the planet, in a place called Astrosaurs Academy."

"Excellent!" boomed Inferniak. "We shall fry all the dinos of this world with our lava-lasers. Then we shall wake our sleeping armies and conquer all—"

Suddenly, a small explosion sent a tingle through the ship, closely followed by another – and another. "Under attack," grated the volcano-men. "Under attack!"

"Small airborne vehicles are crashing into the sides of our ship," the chief reported.

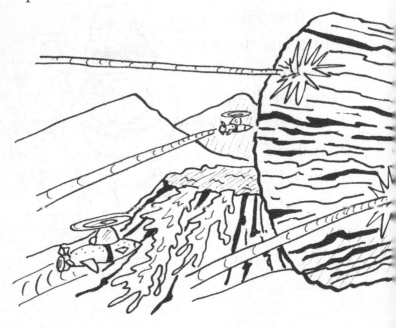

"Who dares to defy us?" Inferniak bellowed, his voice echoing through the gigantic control room as his warriors checked their glowing instruments. "They must be found – and obliterated at once! Find them! NOW!"

In the flight deck of the astro-carrier, still hovering above the shaking, icy sea, the cadets, the commander and the carnivores watched the little vessels strike the volcano.

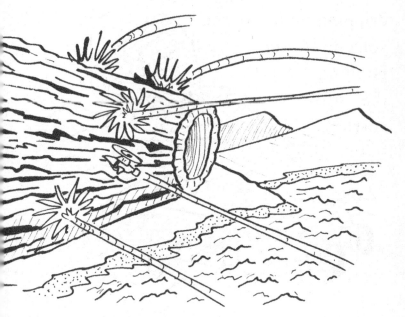

"Fifteen brand-new training vehicles," sighed Gruff.

Erick sniffed. "Bye-bye, lovely heli-subs!"

"The autopilots worked like a dream," Teggs murmured.

Damona nodded. "But will Inferniak even notice?"

"He's noticed all right!" Blink squawked in alarm. "Look, he's turning!"

Sure enough, the gaping lava-dripping mouth of the volcano began pointing towards the astro-carrier.

Dutch stared, transfixed. "Here we go . . ."

"I can't watch!" groaned Splatt.

Teggs looked to the two megalosaurus. "How long before the ice-core goes boom?"

Korlius considered. "Given the size of this ocean and how long it's been since the red leaf-eater threw it away . . ." He started counting on his claws. "I would say, maybe two minutes?"

"Give or take a minute or two," added Tarq.

"Very helpful!" Damona muttered.

Suddenly, an enormous jet of thick, liquid lava came shooting from the mouth of Mount Steamalot. The cadets cried out, the carnivores gasped and even Gruff gave a snort of amazement as Erick quickly reversed the astro-carrier. The deadly, sizzling spurt missed them by a scale's breath and struck the juddering, frozen waves with a hiss of steam.

"That was too close," said Netta shakily.

"Don't reverse any further, Commander Gruff," said Tarq. "Tell your colonel to stay close to the stump of the volcano – that's where the mega ice-maker fell, and where the most exploding sea-slush will be produced."

"I don't take orders from meat-eaters," Gruff retorted – as another huge blast of lava squirted from the volcano ship. "There again, a moving target is harder to hit. Do it, Erick!"

"Aye-aye, Commander!" Erick sent the carrier speeding away as fast as he could towards Volcallid's smoky shores.

"We'll never survive two more minutes of this!"

Splatt moaned as the carrier slowed again.

"We must!" Teggs was so scared and excited he started chewing his tail spikes. "If we fail, millions of dinosaurs will die!"

"The sea is really shaking now!" Damona yelled, pointing through a porthole.

Teggs rushed to see. Sure enough, huge ripples were spreading through the orange ice. The tops of the frozen waves were shattering like glass. "Damona's right. It's going to blow!"

"That volcano ship's almost on top of us!" Netta shouted.

"Hear this, you dismal dinosaurs . . ." Inferniak's scary voice hissed over the ship's speakers. "Our lava-lasers have locked on to your puny craft. There is nowhere to run. Prepare for sizzling destruction!"

"Oh, we're prepared all right," Teggs shouted, as the slush-ice sea began to bubble. "Only it's not *our* sizzling destruction we're ready for – it's YOURS!"

As he spoke, the entire ocean seemed to glow, as though a sun were rising beneath it.

"Time to split!" Erick cried. He gripped the controls and pulled sharply upwards as Inferniak opened fire and then—

SPLA-BOOOOOOM!

The half-frozen ocean erupted with ten times the force that Mount Steamalot could ever muster! Tidal waves of ice as tall as mountains rose up and broke over the volcano ship. Inferniak wailed so loudly he blew every speaker in the astro-carrier: billions of tons of freezing salty sleet flushing through the fiery insides of the volcano-men's craft. As Erick took the astro-carrier higher into the air, out of reach of the carnage, the evil king's flash-frozen spaceship plunged from the sky and struck the surging slush-water with a crash that was off the scale. The waters steamed and smoked and bubbled as the vile volcano sank from sight beneath the angry waves.

For a few seconds, no one in the
carrier dared to say a word, watching
and wondering and
worrying . . .

Then Dutch broke
the silence in typical
style. "*Wooooooo-
HOOO!*"

"We did it!" Teggs
yelled, grabbing
Blink and Dutch in a
bear hug. Damona and
her Darlings did a victory
dance together. Even
Gruff and Erick
couldn't help but
high-five Tarq
and Korlius –
although all
four of them
quickly
controlled
themselves.

Gruff cleared his throat. "All right, cadets," he grumbled. "This has been one of the craziest days I can remember. I shall expect a written report from all of you for the Academy files, explaining everything that's gone on."

Splatt saluted. "Yes, sir."

"I'll call mine 'The Case of the Volcano-NO-NO'!" said Dutch.

Netta gave him a shove. "I'm just glad the report will have a happy ending."

"Your cadets do you credit, Commander," hissed Tarq. "I hope we shall fight them in a war, sometime."

"Praise indeed," said Gruff dryly.

"But what will become of us?" asked Korlius.

Gruff looked sternly at the carnivores. "You know, trespassing on a plant-eater planet is a serious crime."

"Um, sir?" said Blink. "Tarq and Korlius only came to Astro Prime to stop the volcano-men."

Teggs nodded. "And without their ice-maker, Inferniak would be ruling this world by now."

"Our work is not yet done," Tarq said. "There are other volcano ships hidden on other planets that we must find and freeze."

Erick looked at Gruff. "Perhaps we should all work together to take care of them?"

Korlius smiled at Tarq. "Permission to enter plant-eater space would certainly make the task easier."

Damona smiled. "Cool!"

"Freezing, more like!" Blink joked.

"Forget freezing, I'm *famished*!" Teggs declared. "I haven't eaten so much as a blade of grass for hours!"

Gruff smiled. "I guess I can drop you cadets at the canteen while I go and explain to DSS HQ that we're missing a volcano."

"I'm not missing it at all!" said Netta flatly.

"Me neither," Teggs agreed, with a wink at Blink and Dutch. "I have to admit, I never want to see another volcano for as long as I live . . . but I wouldn't have missed a *lava*-ly adventure like that for anything!"

THE END

The cadets of Astrosaurs Academy
will return in
SPACE KIDNAP!

Visit the coolest school in space!

ASTROSAURS ACADEMY

DESTINATION: DANGER!

by Steve Cole

Young Teggs Stegosaur is a pupil at ASTROSAURS ACADEMY — where dinosaurs train to be ASTROSAURS. With his best friends Blink and Dutch beside him, amazing adventures and far-out fun are never far away!

Arriving at the Academy, the new astro-cadets face their first mission — to camp out in a deserted space wilderness and bring back something exciting for show-and-tell. But the sneaky tricks of a rival team mean big trouble for Teggs, Blink and Dutch — especially when a T.rex ship crash-lands close by with a VERY hungry crew . . .

ISBN: 978 1 862 30553 3

Riddle of the Raptors

Available from Feb 2010 with a cool new look!

Astrosaurs
*Riddle of
the Raptors*
By Steve Cole

BLAST OFF!

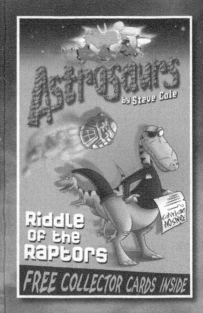

Teggs is no ordinary dinosaur – he's an **Astrosaur**!
Captain of the amazing spaceship DSS *Sauropod*, he goes on
dangerous missions and fights evil – along with his faithful
crew, Gypsy, Arx and Iggy!

When a greedy gang of meat-eating raptors raid the
Sauropod and kidnap two top athletes, Teggs and his crew
race to the rescue. But there's more to the raptors' plot than
meets the eye. Can Teggs solve their rascally riddle in time?

Collect your very own Astrosaurs cards! Included in the back
of each book.

ISBN: 978 0 099 47294 0